A Marc Brown ARTHUR Chapter Book

Arthur
Makes the Team

Little, Brown and Company

Boston   New York   Toronto   London

For Tucker

First Edition

The characters and events portrayed in this book are fictitious. Any
similarity to real persons, living or dead, is coincidental and not
intended by the author.

Text by Stephen Krensky, based on the teleplay by Tom Hertz
Text has been reviewed and assigned a reading level by Laurel S. Ernst,
M.A., Columbia Teachers College, New York, New York;
reading specialist, Chappaqua, New York.

ISBN 0-316-11550-9 (hc)
ISBN 0-316-11551-7 (pb)
Library of Congress Catalog Card Number 97-069736

10 9 8 7 6 5 4 3

WOR (hc)
COM-MO (pb)

Published simultaneously in Canada by Little, Brown & Company
(Canada) Limited

Printed in the United States of America

Chapter 1

Buster and Arthur were walking along the sidewalk with their baseball gloves. As they walked, they tossed a ball back and forth.

"So, do you think you'll be good at baseball?" Buster asked.

Arthur shrugged. "I hope so," he said. He didn't want to admit to being nervous. He hadn't played last year, like some of the other kids.

"Did you learn a lot last year?" he asked.

Buster laughed. "Did I? Let me show you. Run out for a long catch."

Arthur trotted past a tree.

1

Buster waved him on. "Farther . . . farther . . . Okay, stand there. Are you ready? See if you can catch the famous Buster Ball."

"Ready!" said Arthur. He held up his glove.

Buster threw the ball as hard as he could. But instead of going toward Arthur, the ball shot up into a tree. It bounced around in the branches.

"I've got it," said Arthur, circling underneath.

The ball bounced down off one branch, then another, before rolling onto a roof.

"I've still got it," said Arthur, following the ball's every move.

The ball rolled down the roof and into the gutter. It shot out the bottom of the downspout, passed between Arthur's legs, and rolled into a storm drain.

"Oops!" said Arthur. "I guess I don't have it after all."

Buster looked down the drain. He sighed. "I lose more balls that way."

"That was a pretty amazing throw," said Arthur. "And you learned that in just one season?"

"I sure did. Don't worry — you'll catch on quickly. Just think: you're standing out there in the middle of the field. There's no one around."

"No one around," said Arthur.

"No place to hide," said Buster.

"No place to hide," Arthur repeated.

"At the crack of the bat, the ball is headed your way. Everyone is staring, watching your every move."

"My every move?" said Arthur.

"Of course," said Buster. "And not just your teammates. The other team is watching, too. And the crowd in the stands. Especially your family."

"My family?"

Buster nodded. "Sure. Parents. Grandparents. Sisters. Everybody comes to the games."

Arthur sighed. "Let me get this straight. I'm all alone in the middle of the field, and the whole world is watching whenever the ball comes to me."

"Pretty exciting, huh?" said Buster.

"I guess," said Arthur. *Exciting* wasn't actually the word he had in mind.

"And don't forget batting," said Buster.

"No, I wouldn't want to do that."

Buster crouched down in a batting stance. "It's just you and the pitcher. Nothing else matters. You raise your bat. Ready. Waiting. The pitch blazes in. You can feel the heat as the ball passes by."

Arthur swallowed. "You feel the heat?"

"Well, maybe not," Buster admitted. "But it's a tense moment."

"Because everyone is watching."

"Exactly."

"The umpire calls, 'Strike!' But that's

okay. It wasn't your pitch. But now you stand in."

"Stand in," said Arthur.

"It's another fastball. But this time you swing. The ball streaks like a rocket. It's a home run! You circle the bases to the cheers of the crowd."

"Just like that?" said Arthur.

"Well, not every time. But it could happen if you're lucky."

Arthur sighed. He didn't know if that would happen to him. But it was nice to think about.

Chapter 2

. . . .

At the ball field, a bunch of kids were huddled around the bulletin board, looking at the team rosters.

"I found my name," said Buster. "Let's see . . . Francine . . . Brain . . . Binky . . . Arthur. Yes! Yes! We're all on the Eagles together. Hey, this is going to be a great team. I can't wait to start pitching."

"Hey, I want to pitch!" said Francine.

"So do I," said the Brain.

"How will we choose?" asked Buster.

"Don't worry," said Francine. "The coach will decide."

"But Francine," said the Brain, "your father is the coach."

She smiled. "Funny how these things work out."

"How what things work out?" asked her father, coming up to join them. He had on his official Eagles hat and T-shirt.

"Nothing, Daddy," said Francine, smiling at him.

"I think I'm going to be sick," whispered Buster.

"I think you'll have company," the Brain whispered back.

The whole team — including Sue Ellen, Speedy, Fern, and Alex — sat down in the grass.

"I'm glad everyone could be here for our first practice," said the coach. "As most of you know, I'm Oliver Frensky, Francine's dad."

Francine gave Buster a big smile.

"Now, our motto is going to be

'Teamwork!' " the coach went on. "If you have a favorite position, you can start with that. But you'll all be moving around. Who's going to be our first pitcher?"

Buster, Francine, and the Brain all raised their hands.

"Excellent. We have a whole staff. Buster, why don't you go first?"

"But . . . but —," Francine sputtered.

"You'll get your turn," her father reassured her.

Everyone else took a position. Arthur ended up in right field. Nobody else seemed to want to be there.

"Heads up, everyone!" said the coach, waiting with a bat at home plate. "Go ahead, Buster."

Buster prepared to pitch. He twirled his arm around, shot out his leg, and threw as hard as he could.

Coach Frensky blinked.

"Where did the ball go?"

Buster wasn't sure. He was never sure with a Buster Ball. A moment later the ball came down and hit him on the head.

"Are you all right, Buster?" asked the coach.

Buster nodded.

"Good. Try again. But this time ease up a little. Don't wear your arm out the first day."

Buster nodded. He pitched again — and the ball sailed right over the plate. The coach lined a drive to Sue Ellen at third base.

After a few more pitches, it was Francine's turn. Her first pitches were high and outside. Her father fouled them off.

"Nice energy," he said. "Remember now, right over the plate."

Francine's next pitches were better. Her father batted them around the field.

Time for my fastball, thought Francine.

She gripped the ball firmly — and threw.

The ball sailed high over everything — her father, Binky, even the backstop.

"Well," said her father, "that was certainly over the plate."

"Way over," said Binky.

The coach cleared his throat. "All right, Francine, let's give someone else a chance."

The Brain took to the mound.

"Ready?" asked the coach.

"In a moment," said the Brain. He licked his finger and held it up to test the wind direction. Then he began scraping the mound with his sneaker.

"Is everything all right?" asked the coach.

"Oh, yes," said the Brain. "Proper footing is very important."

When he was finally ready, the Brain made his first careful pitch.

Coach Frensky hit a grounder to short-stop.

The Brain was pleased. He checked the wind and his footing again. He did that before every pitch, so he didn't get many in.

The last ball went to right field. It was a deep pop fly.

"I've got it!" said Arthur, moving backward. He leaped at what he thought was the right moment.

And missed.

The ball came down behind him.

"Almost!" said the coach. "Arthur, that was a very graceful leap."

Graceful? Aurthur didn't feel graceful. He could feel his face getting red. He knew everyone was looking at him.

It was starting to look like the season would be a long one.

Chapter 3

• • • • • • • • • • • •

Arthur stood in front of his bedroom mirror, tossing a ball up and down in his mitt.

His father stopped in the hall to watch him. "Ready for your next practice, Arthur?" he asked.

Arthur dropped the ball. "Oh, uh . . . yeah," he said.

Mr. Read stepped into the room. "Is everything okay?"

"Um, I guess. Practices have been hard."

"Really? Tell me about them."

"I'm not very comfortable yet. The other day I was playing second base. I fielded a sharp grounder, but I couldn't get it out of my glove. It was like the ball was stuck with glue."

"What did you do?" his father asked.

"Well, there was a force on at second, so I took off the glove and threw it to the shortstop, who was covering the bag."

"Was the throw in time?"

Arthur sighed. "The glove was. But the ball came out along the way and dribbled into the outfield. The runner ended up at third base."

"What did the coach say?" asked Mr. Read.

"He said I was ingenious. Very creative. He uses words like that a lot when I make a play."

Mr. Read sat down on the bed. "The coach has a good eye, Arthur. You just need to give it a little time."

Arthur wasn't so sure. "Everyone else just seems so far ahead of me. And I feel funny asking for help about stuff that everybody else knows already."

"Yes, well, most of them played last year, and you didn't. Having a head start makes a difference. I had kind of the same thing happen to me."

"You did?"

His father nodded. "It was when I first got interested in cooking. Of course, I didn't know I would end up as a caterer. I just liked experimenting with food. I was sick the first week and missed the class where the teacher explained how all the equipment worked. The next week I was too shy to ask questions. I just pretended I knew as much as everyone else."

"Did it work?" asked Arthur.

His father smiled. "For a few minutes. But then we had to make salad dressing in a blender. Everyone else knew that the lid needed to be locked a certain way. I didn't. So when I turned it on . . ."

Arthur gasped.

"You guessed it. The salad dressing ended up on everything and everyone else. It was quite a mess."

"Did you get in trouble?"

His father made a face. "For a moment I thought my life was over. The teacher was covered in goop. He shook his fist at me, and goop dropped off his hand onto the floor."

Arthur's mouth dropped open.

"The room was perfectly still. And then he started to laugh. 'This,' he said, 'is a good example of what I was talking about — *last week.*' "

Arthur sighed. "So you survived."

"Exactly. But I never tried to pretend I knew what I was doing again. And you shouldn't, either. Don't be afraid to ask for help or advice. You'll catch up soon enough."

Chapter 4

. . . .

Coach Frensky was standing behind the backstop, watching his team warm up.

"Excuse me. Coach?"

The coach turned.

"I'm Buster's mother, Bitsy."

"Nice to meet you. Buster's a fine boy, a real sparkplug!"

"That's very nice to hear. I was just wondering . . . Is the ball very hard?"

"Well, no harder than any baseball."

"I see. I've just been wondering . . . What if it hits Buster?"

"Well, there's always some risk, but Buster's very quick. I'm sure —"

"And the baseball hats, are they made of wool? I think Buster's allergic to wool. If he's scratching, I don't think he'll be playing his best."

"We'll watch for scratching." Coach Frensky glanced at the bleachers. "Now, I'd recommend you find a seat, um, Bitsy. You don't want all the good ones to be taken."

"Do the seats often fill up for practice?"

Coach Frensky hesitated. "You never know," he said.

On the field, Arthur and Buster were throwing to each other. As Francine approached, Buster held up an imaginary microphone in front of her mouth.

"Excuse me, Slugger. Buster here for Action News. Think you'll top your record of forty-nine sky balls today?"

"Very funny," said Francine. "At least my throws go over the plate."

"Take it easy," said Arthur. "You're both on the same team, remember?"

"Stay out of this, Arthur," said Francine. "You need to concentrate all your attention on holding on to the ball."

"Oh, yeah?" Arthur put his hands on his hips — and the ball dropped out of his glove.

Francine laughed and moved onto the field.

"You know what you need, Arthur?" said Buster. "My never-fail, always-succeeds, one-hundred-percent guaranteed, secret good-luck charm."

He reached into his pocket and produced a shriveled carrot.

Arthur made a face.

"Use this and you can't miss," said Buster. He handed the carrot to Arthur.

"You're sure about this?" asked Arthur.

"One hundred percent absolutely double-sure guaranteed."

"Okay," said Arthur, and he put it in his pocket.

All during practice, Arthur fingered the good-luck charm. But since no tough balls were hit to him, he couldn't be sure if it was working. When Francine came up to bat, he crouched down to be ready.

Francine crushed the next pitch to deep right field. Arthur ran back, watching it the whole way.

"Watch the fence!" Buster yelled.

Arthur stopped short and looked up. The ball was coming down. He reached out to catch it.

The ball bounced off his glove and went over the fence.

"Home run!" shouted Francine, rounding the bases.

Arthur frowned.

Later, Arthur returned the carrot to Buster.

"Here," he said. "I think it's broken. Or maybe it's run out of luck."

Then he walked away.

Buster examined the carrot and shrugged. He took a bite and put the rest in his pocket.

Chapter 5

• • • • • • • • • • • •

After practice, Coach Frensky led the team to the Sugar Bowl.

"You've been working hard," he said. "Time for a little reward."

Arthur was the last in, just behind Buster. It was amazing to him that everyone else could be so happy and relaxed. Most of the kids had made the same kind of mistakes on the field that he had. Somehow it didn't seem to bother them so much.

"A great practice deserves ice cream!" said the coach. He went off to see about getting some tables pushed together.

"Are you prepared, Arthur?" Francine asked.

Arthur eyed her cautiously. "What do you mean?"

"An ice cream cone can be tricky. If you're not careful, you might drop it."

A lot of the kids laughed.

"Don't listen to her, Arthur," said Buster. "You're entitled to ice cream just as much as the rest of us. If you want, though, I'll hold it for you."

"Thanks, Buster," said Arthur. "I think."

Once their orders were taken, everyone sat down. Arthur, Francine, Buster, the Brain, and Binky were all at the same table.

Francine was busy complaining. "Our problem is batting," she said. "We don't have good batting."

Arthur had struck out twice that afternoon. He was swinging too soon, the coach had told him.

"I think we look pretty good," said Buster.

Francine laughed. "With your eyesight, I'm not surprised."

"There's nothing wrong with my eyesight," said Buster. "I eat plenty of carrots."

Arthur fiddled with his glasses. Sometimes it was hard to keep his eye on the ball.

"Some people," said Binky, "have to learn how to stop the ball." He pounded his chest. "Even if you can't keep it in your glove, you keep it in front of you."

Arthur looked down at his legs. Balls had passed through them so often, they felt like goalposts.

"If we concentrate on learning the fundamentals," said the Brain, "our chances of winning will improve over time."

"I suppose," said Francine. "But they don't look too good right now."

"Well," said the Brain, "it would help if you stopped throwing the ball over Fern's head."

"I didn't do that!" said Francine. "And she was standing too close, anyway."

Coach Frensky arrived at the table with two pitchers of soda.

"Hey!" he said, frowning. "I don't want to hear any talk like that. We're a team, remember?"

Everyone shut up.

Coach Frensky surveyed the table. "Where's Arthur?" he asked.

"He was here a second ago," said Buster.

"Probably went for napkins," said Binky.

"Look!" said the Brain. He pointed out the window.

Arthur was slinking up the street. A line of drips from his ice cream cone trailed behind him.

"I guess he wasn't in the mood for talk," said Francine.

"I guess not," said her father. But he stood there thinking it over for a long time.

Chapter 6

At dinner, Arthur sat quietly at the table. He barely touched his hamburger. He wasn't very hungry.

The same could not be said for D.W. Her hamburger was half gone, and she was munching away on corn-on-the-cob.

"I see you favor the rolling approach," said her father.

D.W. looked confused. "What's that?"

"It's when you roll your corn around before moving it down a little and rolling it some more."

D.W. stopped to look at her corn. "It's the best way," she said.

"Don't be so sure," said her mother. "Some people favor the typewriter approach — eating all the way across in a row, turning the cob a little, and then starting a new row."

D.W. shrugged. "My way is better," she said.

"For you, sweetie," said her mother.

"What do you think, Arthur?" asked Mr. Read.

"Huh?"

Arthur hadn't been listening.

"Which way do you like to eat corn?" his father asked.

Arthur sighed. "Whichever way you make the fewest mistakes."

Mr. Read looked confused. "I'm not sure you can make a mistake eating corn," he said. "True, you could miss a kernel here or there, but I'm not sure that really counts."

"Arthur's not talking about corn," said D.W. "He's talking about baseball."

"How are your practices going?" asked his mother.

"Not too well," said Arthur. "I know what to do in my head. But my body doesn't always go along."

"That's perfectly natural," said Mr. Read. "Be patient, Arthur. You're paying attention, and that's what's important. Baseball is ninety-nine percent concentration."

"Sometimes it feels like everyone is concentrating on what a bad job I'm doing. Not Coach Frensky, though. He's always encouraging. He says I'm making good progress."

"Which parts do you feel comfortable with?" asked his mother.

Arthur stopped to think. "I can throw okay. And when the ball is hit to me, I can get to the right place . . ."

"But you can't catch the ball," said D.W.

"D.W.!" said her father. "You'll catch

more than a ball if you say another word."

D.W. went back to her corn.

Arthur stared at his plate. "She's right," he said. "It's what everyone else says."

"Nonsense," said Mr. Read. "I'm sure you're making a positive contribution. There are probably people talking about it even now."

"You really think so?"

Mr. Read nodded. "Absolutely. So you'd better eat up. Ballplayers need their strength."

Arthur nodded. With their first game coming up, he wanted to be ready. He picked up his corn in both hands. With a look at D.W., he began eating it across in rows.

Chapter 7

• • • • • • • • • • •

"It's painful," Francine was saying.

She was sitting in her living room with Muffy.

"What's painful?" Muffy asked. "No, don't tell me. It has something to do with baseball."

Francine was surprised. "How did you know?" she asked.

"Because that's all you talk about lately. Double plays . . . making the cutoff . . . guarding the plate."

"Well, it's important," said Francine.

Muffy yawned. "Not to me. I could

understand it better if you thought your team was any good."

Francine punched her pillow. "Don't remind me. Buster can't throw. The Brain takes too long for everything. And as for Arthur . . ." She shook her head.

"Couldn't you promote him or something?" said Muffy. "Make him president or general manager? Anything to get him off the field. My daddy's always talking about people getting kicked upstairs in business."

Francine hadn't thought of that. "It might work. We could give Arthur lots of interesting jobs. He'd be really busy."

"Give him a fancy title and some fringe benefits," said Muffy. "You know, like free parking and paid vacations. My daddy says those are important."

Francine was nodding. "Yes, yes," she said. "Arthur would probably like all that."

"Arthur would probably like *what?*" asked her father, coming in from the kitchen.

"We were just discussing the team, Daddy."

The coach smiled. "We're pulling together nicely," he said. "Still a few kinks, of course, but that's only normal."

Francine smiled at him. "Speaking of kinks, Daddy, Muffy suggested a way to get Arthur off the field: promote him to assistant coach."

"Oh, really?" said Mr. Frensky.

Francine folded her fingers together. "What do you say, Daddy? Please! I can't even throw straight because I'm worrying what dumb thing Arthur's going to do next."

"That sounds serious," said her father. "You're worried about Arthur, aren't you?"

"Why, yes . . . Can't you see that?"

Her father stroked his chin. "It's natural

for you to be concerned. After all, he is one of your best friends."

"Then you'll do it?"

Her father thought for a moment. "As coach, I have to look beyond any one player's needs. I have to consider the whole team."

"Of course," said Francine. "I think the whole team would benefit."

"You have to stand way back to get the big picture," said her father. "I may not have been seeing everything myself. Thank you, Francine."

"So you'll promote him?"

Her father shook his head. "No, no, I've got a better idea."

"Oh?" Francine didn't want a better idea. She liked her idea just the way it was.

Her father rubbed his chin. "Yes . . . definitely a better idea. I'm not going to promote Arthur. I'm going to promote you instead."

"What? You mean you want to get me off the field?"

"Not exactly," said her father, grinning broadly. "I had a different promotion in mind."

Francine looked at him suspiciously. Whenever her father used that tone, something odd was bound to happen.

Chapter 8

● ● ● ● ● ● ● ● ● ● ● ●

Arthur stood in his garage, throwing a tennis ball against the wall.

Bounce-bounce-catch.

Bounce-bounce-catch.

Too bad they don't use these in the games, he thought.

"Hi, Arthur."

Francine stood in the driveway.

Arthur ignored her.

Bounce-bounce-catch.

Bounce-bounce-catch.

"Come on, Arthur. You can't ignore me forever."

Arthur stopped bouncing the ball.

"What brings you here, Francine? No, don't tell me. I'll bet you've thought up some new insults since yesterday."

Francine's face reddened. "Actually, I came over with some news. My father has made me the new assistant coach."

"Congratulations. Would that be Assistant Coach in Charge of Criticism?"

"No, no . . . Look, Arthur, maybe I have gotten a little carried away lately. I'm sorry. But now my dad says I have to make sure the team works together."

She took out a baseball.

"And my first project is you."

"Me?" Arthur crossed his arms. "What if I don't want to be a project?"

"Would you rather be teased and feel embarrassed all the time?"

Arthur sighed. He picked up his glove, and they went into the backyard.

"Ready?" said Francine.

She threw the ball high overhead.

Arthur circled underneath it. "I've got it! I've got it!"

The ball landed five feet away.

Francine smothered a giggle. "Let's try again," she said.

She picked up the ball and threw it up into the air.

Arthur raised his glove.

"That's it," said Francine. "Get under it!"

Arthur followed the ball's path — until the sun blinded him. He raised his arm to block the sun — and the ball hit him on the head.

"Ouch!"

"Well," said Francine, "at least you were under it. Look." She came over to show him. "Use your glove to keep the sun out of your eyes. That also puts the glove in a better place to catch the ball. Don't think about doing everything at once. Break it into steps."

"Oh," said Arthur. "I see."

"One more time . . ."

She threw the ball up again. This time Arthur used his glove to block the sun. He circled and circled — and caught the ball.

Arthur smiled.

Francine smiled, too.

They practiced a few more times.

"I think you're getting the hang of this, Arthur."

He thought so, too.

"Thanks, Francine. You know, you might take a little advice yourself."

"Me? About what?"

"About pitching your fastball." He crouched down into a catching stance. "Come on, fire it in here."

Francine threw the ball. It sailed over Arthur's head, Pal's doghouse, and the fence.

While Francine went to get the ball, Arthur stopped to think.

"All right," said Francine, returning to her position. "Let's try again."

"Wait a minute," said Arthur. "You know, Francine, maybe you should think about your pitching the same way you told me to think about my catching?"

"What do you mean?"

"Breaking it into steps. Look, when you throw, you need to push off with your legs first and use your shoulder. And even after you release the ball, you still have to follow through."

"How do you know so much about it?"

Arthur looked a little embarrassed.

"Well?"

"Actually, it was D.W. I heard her explaining the whole thing to my mother."

"You're telling me to take advice from D.W.?"

Arthur shrugged. "Nobody has to know — especially D.W. What have you got to lose?"

"All right," said Francine. She got ready. "Legs . . . shoulder . . ."

She fired the ball in at Arthur.

"Ouch!" he shouted. He pulled his hand out of his glove and shook it. "That was a real fastball."

Francine looked pleased. "It was, wasn't it?" she said. "Thanks for the tip."

"You're welcome," said Arthur.

Francine paused. "I really am sorry I teased you so much before."

Arthur nodded. "Well, you do overdo it sometimes."

"If I ever overdo it again, let me know. Deal?"

"Deal."

"It was kind of your fault, though."

"My fault?" said Arthur. "How do you figure that?"

"Well, if you hadn't kept dropping balls, I wouldn't have teased you."

"Oh, yeah? Well at least when I throw a ball, it lands in the same neighborhood."

As Francine started to answer, she suddenly froze — and laughed.

Arthur laughed, too. "Here we go again . . . ," he said.

Chapter 9

• • • • • • • • • • •

Coach Frensky paced back and forth in front of his bench. "Okay, team, this is our first game. The Penguins are pretty good, I hear." He took a deep breath. "But I want you to play just the way you have in practice. Just go out and have fun."

The coach clapped his hands. "Okay, team. Let's go!"

The Eagles took the field. In the first inning, a ball was hit sharply on the ground to Arthur. He fielded it cleanly and threw to second base.

"All right, Arthur!" said Buster.

His parents cheered from the bleachers.

"That's my brother," D.W. told everyone around her. "I taught him everything he knows."

The next four innings passed quickly. Each team scored two runs. In the bottom of the fifth, Arthur came up to bat for the second time. He had walked before.

Now he rapped a single to center.

"Way to go, Arthur!" yelled Francine from the bench.

Buster was next. He fouled off two pitches but swung all the way around on the third.

"Strike three!" shouted the umpire.

Mrs. Baxter stood up in the stands and clapped. "Way to swing, Buster!" she called out.

The Brain pitched the last two innings. The sixth was scoreless, but in the top of the seventh, the Penguins scored a run to take the lead. Then, with two outs, their fifth batter singled to first and reached third on an overthrow.

The next batter came up.

The Brain licked his finger, testing the wind direction.

Then he threw to the plate.

Thwack!

It was a deep fly ball.

"It's yours, Arthur," Francine called from second base.

"I can't watch," said Buster in left field.

Arthur backpedaled over the grass. He blinked a few times, but he never took his eye off the ball. Remember what Francine said, he told himself. He shielded his eyes with his glove.

Arthur reached the fence. The ball was coming down fast.

Plopp.

Arthur had caught it.

"Relay!" shouted Francine.

Arthur threw the ball. Francine caught it and spun around. The runner had tagged up at third and was heading for home plate.

Binky was waiting.

"Throw it!" he called out.

Francine wasn't pitching, but she knew she had to throw a perfect fastball. She planted her feet firmly and fired to him.

The runner was sliding in. Binky swept him with the tag.

"Out!" called the umpire.

Arthur's team trotted in from the field. They were down one run, but they still had their last turn at bat.

The game wasn't over yet.

Chapter 10

• • • • • • • • • • • •

Everyone on the bench was watching the field.

Sue Ellen was up first. The first pitch was a ball.

"Wait for yours!" shouted Francine.

Sue Ellen nodded. She stepped back into the batter's box.

In came the pitch.

Sue Ellen swung hard — and lined the ball into left field.

Coach Frensky whistled. "All right! The tieing run's on first."

Fern was the next batter. She hit a

blooper to right field, advancing Sue Ellen to second.

"Keep it going," said the coach.

Now Binky came to the plate. He tapped the dirt from his cleats and cocked his bat.

In came the pitch.

Binky swung hard, but a little early. The ball went deep to right field, but it was caught just before the fence. He was out, but Sue Ellen tagged up at second and ran to third.

Buster was up next.

"Just make good contact," said the coach. "A single ties it. Keep us alive."

Buster nodded.

He watched the first two pitches pass. One ball and one strike.

The third pitch came in. Buster jumped on it.

The ball popped up a mile high. Everyone looked up.

The pitcher called for the catch.

Arthur held his breath. Maybe the pitcher would trip on the grass or be blinded by the sun or get a sudden itch in his back and scratch it with his glove.

Thummp!

The ball was caught. The game was over. The Penguins had won.

Buster trudged back to the dugout as the other team ran off the field, cheering in victory.

"Good effort, Buster," said the coach. "I thought that one was heading for the fence."

"Me, too," said Arthur. "Good try."

Francine stormed over to Buster. "Boy, Buster, all we needed was one little hit, and you couldn't —"

Arthur coughed.

Francine looked at him. "— and you couldn't . . . have made a better try. Good job."

She patted Buster on the shoulder.

Their families gathered round for a few minutes before everyone headed home.

Arthur, Francine, and Buster were the last to leave. They replayed the whole game in their minds.

"We really did pretty well," said Arthur. "And the season's just starting."

"That's right," said Francine. "The next game will be better."

Buster shrugged. "I hope so," he said.

"You know, Buster," said Arthur, "Francine gave me some baseball tips the other day. Maybe she could do the same for you."

"I don't know . . . ," said Buster.

"Just think about all the power you put into your Buster Ball," said Francine.

Buster brightened.

"We just need to find a way to get that

power into your bat. We'll have to get together and —"

"What about now?" Buster asked.

"Now?" Francine looked around. The field was empty.

Buster grabbed a bat and went to home plate. "Come on, come on, what are you waiting for?"

"Arthur?" whispered Francine.

"Yes?"

"Thanks for stopping me before I teased Buster the way I teased you."

"You're welcome. And thanks for helping me with my game. See? Teamwork is the answer."

Francine nodded. "Yeah. But you know, soccer season is coming up. And if you stink at that, I get to tease you all over again."

With that, she went to the pitcher's mound, leaving Arthur to go behind the plate.

"All right, Buster, pay attention. First thing we do . . ."

Arthur smiled. He wouldn't say that Francine would *never* learn.

But it definitely was going to take some time.